The Hippo who was Happy

Designer: Fiona Hajée

Consultant: Cecilia A. Essau, Professor of Developmental
Psychopathology at Roehampton University

Copyright © QED Publishing 2012

First published in the UK in 2012 by
QED Publishing
A Quarto Group Company
230 City Road
London EC1V 2TT

www.qed-publishing.co.uk

A catalogue record for this book is available from
the British Library.

ISBN 978 1 84835 847 8

Printed in China

The Hippo who was Happy

Rachel Elliot
John Bendall-Brunello

QED Publishing

"Bored, bored, BORED!"
said Hippo.

He didn't want
to help Mummy
gather food.

He didn't feel like
sunbathing with Daddy.

"There's nothing to do," he grumbled.

"I'm fed up."

"You can do a special job for me," said Mummy.

"I've picked a juicy water plant
for your Aunty. Will you take it to her?"

"If you like," said Hippo.

Aunty lived on the other
side of the jungle.

Hippo stomped through the tangly undergrowth.

STOMP! STOMP! STOMP!

The noise made him feel a little bit better.

Aunty was having a mud bath.

"Thank you for the water plant," she said.
"Would you like to wallow in the mud with me?"

Aunty showed Hippo how to blow
fountains of mud into the air.

Hippo's fountain went
as high as Aunty's!

Then Aunty pulled herself out
of the mud with a **loud**

SLURRRRP!

"I've got some crunchy roots for my friend Giraffe," she said. "Will you take them to him?"

"If you like," said Hippo.

Giraffe was picking leaves from the tallest trees.

"Thank you for the roots," he said.
"Would you like to pick leaves with me?"

Giraffe showed Hippo how giraffes lean on trees and reach for the leaves with their lips.

When Hippo reached up, the leaves tickled his lips and made him giggle!

Then Giraffe found a twig packed with berries.
"My friend Monkey would like these,"
he said. "Will you take them to her?"

"If you like," said Hippo.

Monkey lived in a tall tree beside the river.
She was swinging from branch to branch.

"Thank you for the berries," she said.
"Would you like to play with me?"

"I'd LOVE to!" said Hippo.

Monkey and Hippo played
games all afternoon.

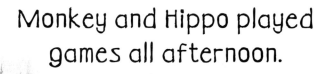

They bellyflopped
into the river.

They rolled down
the grassy banks.

They shared the berries and
splashed the lazy crocodiles.

The sun sank lower
and lower in the sky.

"It's time for me to
go home," said Hippo.

When Hippo got home, Mummy and Daddy were waiting.
They all munched on juicy grass.

"Have you had a happy day?" asked Mummy.
Hippo thought hard.

"I was bored at first," he said.
"But then I started doing things
with my friends...

I blew mud fountains
with Aunty.

I stretched
for leaves
with Giraffe.

I played games
with Monkey.

It's been a **BRILLIANT** day."

"It's not over yet!" said Daddy.
And they all jumped into the cool lake together.

Next steps

- Look at the front cover of the book together. Ask your child to name all the animals in the book: hippo, giraffe, crocodiles and monkey.

- Discuss the shape and colour of each animal, where they live and what they eat.

- Talk to your child about hippos and tell them what they are good at. This would be a good time to explain some of the terms used in the book such as 'wallow in the mud', 'blow fountains of mud into the air' and 'tangly undergrowth'. Discuss what a mud bath is.

- Ask your child what Hippo did first to make himself feel a little bit better.

- Discuss with your child the different types of plants that appear in the book: water plants, undergrowth, trees with berries and grass.

- What did Monkey and Hippo do that made them happy?

- Ask your child why Hippo felt bored. Can they remember what Hippo's mother suggested he did after hearing he was bored?

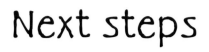

From bored to happy...

- Discuss with your child how Hippo managed to go from feeling bored to feeling happy.

- Ask your child to draw a picture of a child feeling bored and a picture of another child feeling happy. Then ask them why they think some children may sometimes feel bored or sometimes feel happy. Discuss what they could do to avoid feeling bored, and what they could do in order to feel happy.

- Emphasize to your child that there are lots of things they can do when they feel bored. They could help other people, play with other children or try a new activity they have never tried before.